Wolf and Bear

Kate Rolfe

TWO HOOTS

Wolf and Bear were the best of friends.

They played together in the falling leaves,

and paddled in the stream.

But sometimes a great heaviness would fall over Bear,
and the shadow of the mountain would draw him away.

Every day Wolf would check
on Bear and bring him gifts.

"Hey Bear," she called,
"Will you come out of the
shadow and play today?"

"No," said Bear.

"Let's catch the
fluttering leaves!"

"Let's splash in the
sparkling stream!"

"Let's tumble in the
yummy berry bushes!"

"Bear?"

"NO."

"Look Bear! It's snowing!

Let's skate!

Let's skid!

Let's slide!

Let's make blizzards of glittering snowflakes!

Come on, Bear, what do you say?"

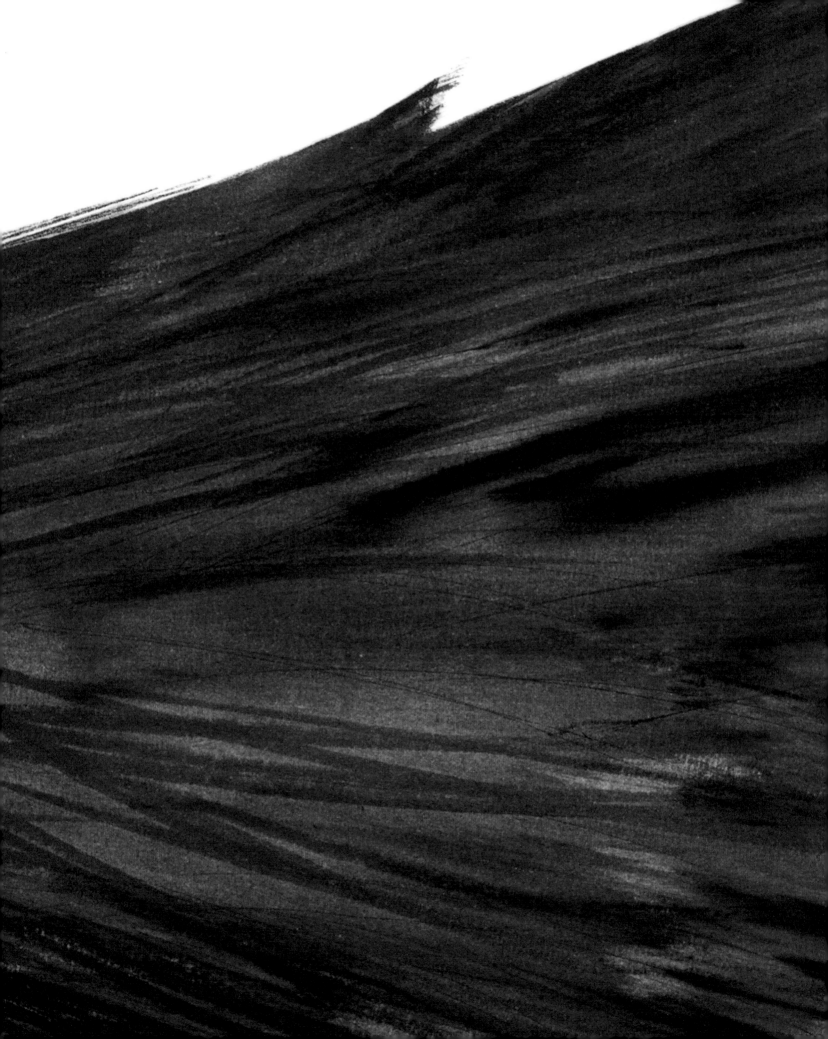

Slowly,

sadly,

Wolf slunk away.

Over time, the shadow drew heavy around Bear, like a cloak.

Wolf walked and walked,

but nowhere felt like

home without Bear.

She sang her sorrows

to a big, bright moon.

The song drifted down,

deep into the shadow.

Bear's ears pricked.
It was the most beautiful
sound he had ever heard.

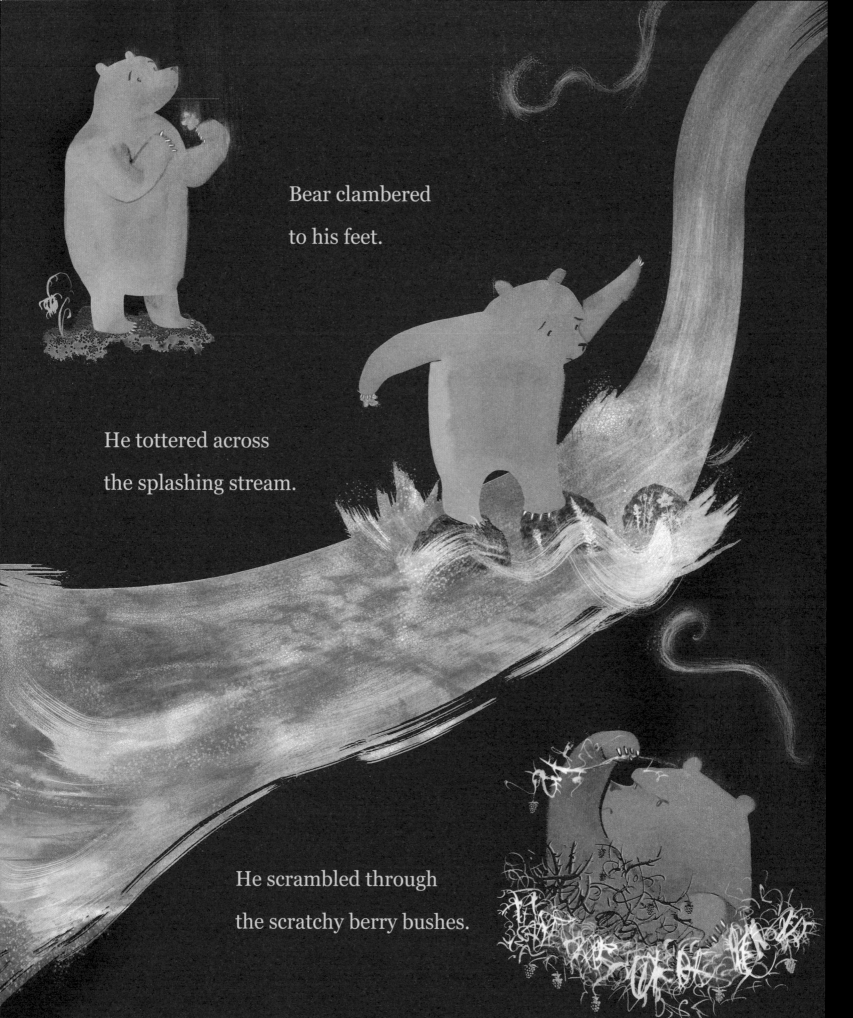

Bear clambered
to his feet.

He tottered across
the splashing stream.

He scrambled through
the scratchy berry bushes.

Then he climbed up and UP!

Finally, Bear reached the point
where the shadow ran out.

He squinted into the light beyond.

It was too bright! He turned away.

This is where his journey

would have to end.

But then . . .

"Arrrrrrooooooooooooooooo"

The song came again, just beyond
the edge of the shadow.
Carefully, Bear stepped into
the light, and saw . . .

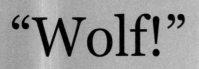

"Wolf!"

"I've missed you," said Bear.

"I've missed you too, Bear," said Wolf.

"Would you like to play?"

"No," said Bear.

"But we could sit together and I could listen to you sing."

So that is what they do.

Whenever a bright moon rises over the mountain,

Bear slips out of the shadow to hear Wolf's song . . .

. . . and she sings

it just for Bear.

for all of us who walk through the shadows,
and those true friends who walk beside us.

The illustrations in this book were created using cyanotype
printmaking — a technique of painting with sunlight and shadow,
which I chose to echo the emotions in the story. The colour
was added with crayon, pastel, and digital drawing.

First published 2023 by Two Hoots an imprint of Pan Macmillan, The Smithson, 6 Briset Street, London EC1M 5NR
EU representative: Macmillan Publishers Ireland Limited, 1st Floor, The Liffey Trust Centre, 117-126 Sheriff Street Upper, Dublin 1, D01 YC43
Associated companies throughout the world
www.panmacmillan.com
ISBN 978-1-0350-1957-1
Text and illustrations copyright © Kate Rolfe, 2023
Moral rights asserted.

www.twohootsbooks.com

MIX
Paper | Supporting
responsible forestry
FSC
www.fsc.org
FSC® C116313

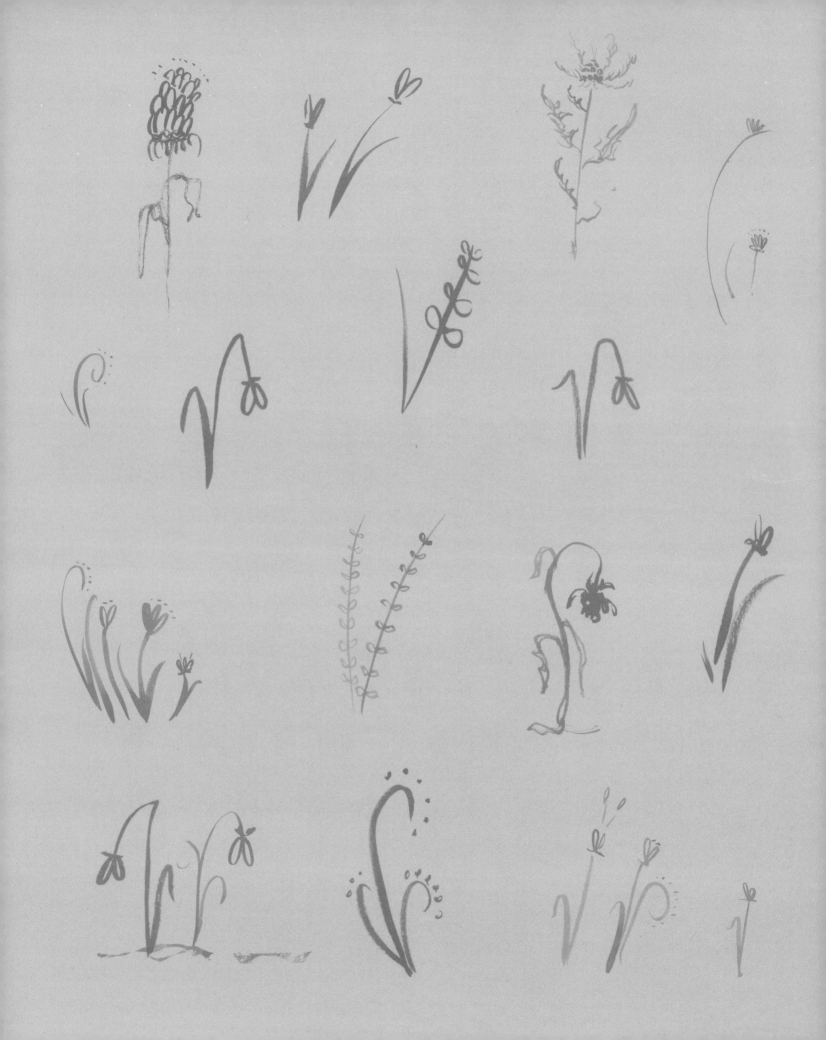